The Trouble with Twins

Other Books by Martha Freeman

1,000 Reasons Never to Kiss a Boy

Who Stole Halloween?

Who Is Stealing the 12 Days of Christmas?

The Trouble with Babies

The Trouble with Cats

The Spy Wore Shades

The Polyester Grandpa

Fourth Grade Weirdo

The Year My Parents Ruined My Life

Stink Bomb Mom

The Trouble with Twins

by Martha Freeman

illustrated by
Cat Bowman
Smith

Holiday House / New York

Text copyright © 2007 by Martha Freeman
Illustrations copyright © 2007 by Cat Bowman Smith
All Rights Reserved
Printed in the United States of America
www.holidayhouse.com
First Edition
1   3   5   7   9   10   8   6   4   2
Library of Congress Cataloging-in-Publication Data
Freeman, Martha, 1956–
The trouble with twins / by Martha Freeman :
illustrated by Cat Bowman Smith. — 1st ed.
p. cm.
Summary: When teenaged Holly takes charge of a birthday
celebration for her two-year-old twin brothers, she gets
more than she bargains for in mayhem, madness, and mess.
ISBN-13: 978-0-8234-2025-4 (hardcover)
ISBN-10: 0-8234-2025-6 (hardcover)
[1. Twins—Fiction.   2. Birthdays—Fiction.
3. Family life—Fiction.]   I. Smith, Cat Bowman, ill. II. Title.

PZ7.F87496Tr2007
[Fic]—dc22   2006041195

For the twins,
Alex and Kyle Poorman,
and their sister,
Courtney
M. F.

The
Trouble
with Twins

Chapter 1

It was only a week till the twins' birthday. Mom was all stressed out.

"I'm so busy!" she told me. "And now Jeremy's getting sick. He was up half the night."

We were in the basement on a Saturday morning. Mom was jogging on her treadmill. Lately Mom is a nut about exercise. It's because she got so fat being pregnant. She said other women look like beach balls; she looked like a circus tent.

"Jeremy's coughing woke me up," I said.

Mom wiped sweat off her forehead. "I'm sorry."

I put on my suffering face. "I'm used to it. It's been almost two years. It's like we've *always* had twins."

Mom was breathing hard. Between breaths, she said, "I'd really like to do something for their second birthday. We kind of skipped over the first one. We were all too tired."

"Did I have a first birthday party?" I asked.

"Oh yeah," Mom said. "Your dad and I were still married, you know. There was a clown. We have pictures somewhere."

"I don't remember," I said.

Mom pressed a button. The treadmill slowed to a stop. She stepped off it. She took a drink from her water bottle. "One-year-olds don't care about birthdays," she said.

"Then why did you have a party?" I asked.

"For us," Mom said. "We were celebrating survival."

I was surprised. "You always say I was a perfect baby!"

Mom put her arm around me. "Of course you were, honey. And the twins are perfect, too."

"Uh-oh," I said. "Was I *that* bad?"

Upstairs the kitchen looked like a battlefield. My brothers, Dylan and Jeremy, were eating beets. There were bloodred spots everywhere.

Dylan and Jeremy were laughing. William,

my stepfather, was not laughing. He was on the floor cleaning up beet spatter. Dylan aimed a spoonful of beet at him. Mom tried to grab the spoon, but she was too late; a beet blob hit William's bald spot.

Mom and I giggled. We couldn't help it.

William tried to wipe the beet off his head. It left a pink smear. "Why do we feed them such brightly colored foods?" he asked. "There are plenty of beige foods. What's the matter with oatmeal?"

"Colorful foods have more vitamins," Mom said.

"I don't eat beets," William said. "And I am perfectly healthy."

Max Cat came into the kitchen.

Jeremy yelled, "Ki'y! Ki'y! Ki'y!" Dylan aimed a beet blob at Max's head. Then he saw I was watching. So he ate the beet blob and smiled at me like an angel.

Max sat down and washed his face. He never knew what didn't hit him.

Jeremy and Dylan are identical twins. But I can tell them apart. Jeremy is bigger. His cheeks are chubbier and pinker; his nose is not so pointy.

Dylan's hair sticks up even if you comb it. His eyebrows are darker.

But how I tell them apart is not really by looks. There's something else. It's hard to explain. The two of them are just different.

Jeremy is the fast one. He was born first. He talked first. He walked first. He is always teaching Dylan how to do new stuff—like how to undo the strap on the high chair and escape.

Dylan is the tricky one. He gets in more trouble. Then he gets out of it by being cute—like now, with that angel smile. You might think that means Dylan is a bigger pain than Jeremy, but really he's not. That's because he's also kind of sweet. He likes to stay in your lap and cuddle more.

Usually he would rather hug the cats than chase them.

Of course, other times he aims beet blobs at Max.

The floor was finally clean—kind of. William sat down with his newspaper. I sat down with a bowl of cereal.

George Cat jumped off a chair and rubbed my mom's leg. He only does that if he's hungry. Wilbur Cat walked into the kitchen from the dining room. I wondered where he had been before that. Not in my laundry hamper, I hoped. Did I remember to close it? Uh-oh.

Wilbur's favorite food is socks, especially sweaty socks. But he will taste anything. Now he sampled a spot of beet from the floor. He didn't care that it had vitamins. He didn't like it.

Max meowed hello to George and Wilbur. The meow woke up Boo Cat. He had been sleeping next to the refrigerator. It's warm there where the vent blows out hot air.

Soon all four cats were meowing and circling Mom's ankles. It was a dancing kitty chorus.

Mom had a mug of coffee in her hand. She tried to walk. But walking is not easy in a chorus of cats. She spilled coffee on Max. He must have thought it was a red-hot raindrop. He jumped up on the counter to escape.

William said, "Get down, Max!" and shoved him without looking. Unfortunately he also shoved a juice glass and the sugar bowl.

Glass, bowl, Max—they all fell to the floor in a shower of sugar.

The twins shouted and clapped. They love noise and breakage.

The cats ran for it.

Mom looked at the damage. Then she looked at William. "Did you forget to feed the cats?" she asked him.

"When would I have fed the cats?" William asked. "I've been busy feeding the twins."

Mom folded her arms and frowned.

William got up and fed the cats.

Mom swept up the sugar and the broken things.

"Did I mention I have to go into the office today?" William asked Mom.

"Oh honey. Not today," Mom said. She listed a bunch of errands and chores.

"You know I've got a court date Monday," William said.

"And you know I have a new client, Szechuan Sushi," Mom said.

William is a lawyer who works in a building that looks like a pyramid. My mom is a book-keeper who works at home. We live in San Francisco, the most beautiful city in the world.

William stood up and looked at Mom. "Your income—" he began.

Mom held up her hand. "Don't start."

"Are we supposed to ignore facts?" William

asked. "You're the bookkeeper. You know whose income runs this house."

"I'm the bookkeeper." Mom nodded. "That means I need time to work."

Uh-oh, I thought. Here comes the fight.

Mom and William have been married almost four years. They didn't used to fight very much. But now they do. Sometimes I worry Mom and William will get divorced like Mom and my dad did.

My friend Sylvie says I worry too much.

"I can do some errands on my way home this afternoon," William said.

"Thank you," Mom said.

Oh good. It looked like the fight was off.

Mom turned to me. "Could you clean the boys up, honey? I'm going to pop into the shower."

The twins had been spoon-feeding each other beets. I used to think it was cute when they fed each other. Now I mostly think it's messy.

I was done with my cereal. I got a washcloth from the drawer by the sink. Before the twins, that drawer had napkin rings and candles in it. Lots of other things have changed because of my little brothers, too. Stuffed animals and plastic toys make the living room a maze. Strollers block the front door. I can barely fit in our car because of the car seats. Sometimes I feel like I barely fit in our house.

But the worst thing is potty training. Now every time I use the toilet, I have to take the potty seat off. Also potty videos are on all the time. I think potty videos are gross.

"Sit still," I told Jeremy as I rubbed beet off his face.

"Otay, Hah-wee," he said. The doctor says both Dylan and Jeremy talk very well for their age. But they still don't say some words right.

"All clean," I said, but then I saw red spots behind his ears.

"My tu'n! My tu'n!" Dylan said.

"No snot!" Jeremy argued.

"Yes! You c'ean. I di'ty." Dylan sounded proud to be dirty.

I took a second cloth and started in on Dylan. "C'acker peez?" he asked.

"You don't need a cracker," I said. "You're full to the top with beets."

Dylan scowled. *"Want* c'acker," he said.

"Hold still," I said. "You look like a clown."

Dylan laughed. There is one good thing about

two-year-olds: They think every dumb thing you say is funny.

"*Want* c'acker," Dylan repeated. "*And* duice."

"You're clean," I said. "Now get down and play with Patrick Opossum."

Dylan's stuffed possum had been lying under his high chair. I wiped the beet spots off him and handed him over.

"Want D-D-D!" Jeremy said.

That means DVD.

"Fine," I said. "Which one?"

"Potty!"

"Fine," I said. "But I'm not watching it with you."

I picked up Jeremy and took Dylan by the hand. They both whined. Jeremy wanted to walk like a big boy. Dylan wanted to be carried like a baby. I ignored them and put in the DVD. As soon as the music came on, they lay back in the bean-bag chair. Jeremy sucked his thumb. Dylan sucked Patrick Opossum's tail. They looked sweet, cute, and loveable.

But then I remembered beets all over the kitchen. I remembered Mom and William almost getting into a fight. *Twins,* I thought, is really another word for *trouble.*

Chapter 2

I was doing my homework that afternoon when Wilbur Cat came into my room. He was walking with his head high, proud of himself. There was something in his mouth. It was white.

Uh-oh. Was he bringing me a trophy?

"Wilbur, *what...?*" I started to say.

Then I saw what. The bathroom door is supposed to stay closed, but somebody had left it open. Wilbur the amazing hunter had captured the end of a roll of toilet paper. No wonder he was proud. He thought he had the world's longest snake!

"You are a dumb, dumb kitty," I said. "But I love you anyway."

I made Wilbur open his mouth. I tried to remove the paper. I couldn't get it all. It was too soggy. Is TP toxic to cats?

I tore off the soggy bits and started rolling the rest back. I followed the trail out my door and toward the stairs. I felt like Hansel and Gretel. I climbed over the baby gate at the bottom of the stairs. I climbed over the baby gate at the top of the stairs. All the time I was re-rolling toilet paper.

"What doin', Hah-wee?" Jeremy asked when I walked past the twins' room. He must have just woken up from his nap.

"Rolling up toilet paper," I said.

"Me do," Jeremy said.

"It's kind of a one-person job," I said.

"Me do!" he insisted.

This woke Dylan up. Dylan had no idea what was going on. But he did not want to be left out. "Me do, too," he said, rubbing his eyes.

"Fine," I said. I dropped the roll of paper I had collected. I helped Jeremy out of his bed. His nose was running. I got a tissue and wiped it. He squirmed to get away. Mom was taking him to the doctor later.

I got Dylan out of his bed. He gave me a wet kiss.

In the hall, I handed Jeremy the roll of paper. I pointed at the trail on the floor ahead of us. "Follow that toilet paper," I said. Jeremy didn't roll the paper neatly like I had. He wadded it instead. "Not like that!" I said.

"Gimme!" Dylan said. He grabbed the paper. Jeremy yanked it back. Toilet paper is not sturdy. It tore. It shredded. It turned into TP confetti. Soon my brothers were having a TP confetti war.

I remembered I still had homework.

"Mom!" I yelled.

That night at dinner, Mom asked William if he had picked up George Cat's pills at the vet.

"I thought you were doing that," William said.

"I had to get Jeremy to the doctor," Mom said. "Stop that, Dylan. Peas go in your mouth, not your ears."

"Is Jeremy okay?" William asked.

"Pink medicine," Mom said.

"*I hate pink medsin!*" Jeremy said.

Mom shook her head. I laughed. Boo Cat jumped up into my lap. Boo is always someplace you don't want him to be. Sometimes, though, I think his furry weight feels nice. I let him stay.

"Anyway, Nancy, you've got tomorrow for the vet, don't you?" William said.

Mom put her fork down. "First, William, the vet is not open on Sunday. Second, I have other plans. Third, they are *your* cats."

I stopped eating. So did the twins.

It looked like the fight was back on.

Chapter 3

The next morning Dylan begged for his own "pink medsin."

I strapped him into his high chair. "It's only for sick people," I told him. "You're not sick."

Dylan disagreed. "I sick!"

"I hate pink medsin!" Jeremy said.

"Have some juice," I said.

Mom had stirred medicine into the apple juice in Jeremy's sippy cup. Jeremy wasn't supposed to know. But now he turned the cup over and watched drops fall onto the high chair tray. The drops were pink.

"I hate dis duice!" Jeremy said. He tossed the

cup in the air. The lid came off. Juice splashed everywhere—even on Max Cat.

Max must have thought it was raining again. This time he didn't jump on the counter. He jumped on Dylan's high chair tray. He landed in oatmeal.

"Bad ki'y! Go 'way!" Dylan pushed him. Max wanted to show Dylan he couldn't be bossed around. So before he jumped down, he swished his tail in Dylan's face. When he walked into the dining room, he left oatmeal and brown sugar tracks. At least they were beige.

Jeremy watched Mom cleaning up apple juice and William sponging apple juice off his newspaper. "Di'n't mean to," he said.

"What do you *mean* you didn't mean to?" I said. "You *threw* your cup halfway across the kitchen!"

"Let it go, Holly," Mom said. "Being sick makes him cranky."

I couldn't believe Jeremy wasn't in trouble. If I threw apple juice, I would be grounded for my whole lifetime.

William went back to reading the newspaper. Mom knelt on the floor and wiped up the oatmeal paw prints.

Still reading, William said, "Remember, Nancy. I like two teaspoons of brown sugar."

From the floor, Mom looked up at him. Then she dropped her rag. Then she took a deep breath. Then she stood and stomped out of the kitchen.

William looked up. "Are we out of brown sugar?" he asked.

"Mommy mad," Jeremy said.

"Way mad," Dylan said.

"Oh dear," William said. He got up and followed Mom.

I went to the stove to fix myself a bowl of oatmeal.

When I turned around . . .

Oh no! Escape attempt!

I forgot that Jeremy had shown Dylan how to undo the high chair strap. Now both boys were standing on the seats, teetering.

"Be careful!" I ran across the kitchen. I grabbed Dylan before he fell. But Jeremy—as usual—was quicker. All I could do was break his fall. With a bump, he landed on his shoulders and did a forward roll. He was surprised but not hurt.

Then he decided it was my fault. "Hah-wee d'op me!" he shouted.

"I did not!" I said.

While Jeremy lay on the floor, Wilbur Cat strolled into the kitchen, sniffed Jeremy's toes in their dinosaur socks, and nibbled a free sample. Dylan laughed and pointed.

Jeremy didn't think it was funny.

"Wi'bur bite me!" he yelled.

Wilbur scuttled away.

"How 'bout a D-D-D?" I said.

"Want *book*!" Dylan said.

"Want *duice*!" Jeremy sat up.

"Oh shoot," I said. "You still need medicine."

I put Dylan on the floor. He found Patrick Opossum and stuck Patrick's tail in his mouth. I put Jeremy back into his high chair.

"Stay put or it's timeout," I said, "even if you are sick." I got the medicine bottle from the fridge, read the label, and measured out a teaspoon.

"Open wide," I said.

Dylan opened his mouth. Jeremy clamped his shut.

What now? "Open wide, and I'll . . . I know. I'll give you a chocolate chip."

Jeremy smiled. "Two tokit tips," he said.

"Me too," said Dylan.

I got a step stool and used it to climb to the kitchen counter. Then I stretched to reach the shelf where my mom hides the chocolate chips. Mostly she hides them from William. She says he is getting soft in the tummy.

I ripped the bag open. A few chips spilled on the floor. I called the five-second rule and ate them.

"Medicine first," I said to Jeremy.

"Tips first," Jeremy said.

I folded my arms and frowned. This is my Mom imitation.

Jeremy said, "Otay."

I stuck the spoon in his mouth. He held his breath and turned red. You would have thought it was arsenic. Finally he swallowed. Then he smiled. "Tips now."

I put two on his tray, then knelt to give Dylan his. Before I could stand up, Jeremy had escaped the strap of his high chair again. This time he climbed down feet first. He is a fast learner all right.

"Book now," Jeremy said. "Peez, Hah-wee?"

When Mom and William came back, I had a boy on each knee. I was reading *The Runaway Bunny*.

"I despise that book," Mom said.

Uh-oh. That meant the fight wasn't over. It was more like halftime.

But then William served himself a bowl of oatmeal and served Mom one, too. She said, "Thank you." She took one bite, then looked up. "Jeremy's medicine," she said. "What did I do with—"

"I gave it to him, Mom."

"You *did*?"

"It cost two chocolate chips each."

William said, "I thought we were *out* of chocolate chips."

The mail from yesterday was still on the kitchen table. On top was a new issue of *Good Parent* magazine. There was a birthday cake on the cover. Mom picked up the magazine and sighed. "Wouldn't it be nice to have a party like this one? Boys, how would you like a jungle party?"

"Want take!" Dylan said.

"I'm sure we could get the bakery to copy that cake," William said.

Mom burst into tears. William and I stared. So did the twins. Then they started crying, too.

"What is it, Mom?" I hugged the twins close.

"I don't *want* a bakery cake," she said. "I want a

homemade cake. I want a homemade party. I'm not good at my job anymore. I'm not good at being a mom. I'm not good at *anything*."

William put his arm around her. "There, there, pumpkin," he said. "They won't be two forever."

This was not a good morning. Three-fifths of us were crying.

"Mom?" I said. "I could make them a cake maybe."

"You?"

I nodded. "I mean, what if I did a party for them?"

"That's a lot," Mom said, "even for a girl who can get pink medicine into a two-year-old."

William said, "If Holly's willing—"

"I could get Xavier and Annie to help," I said. Xavier and Annie are my friends who live on my street.

Mom wiped the tears off her face. "Let me think about it," she said.

William winked and gave me a thumbs-up sign. I went back to *The Runaway Bunny*. Mom rinsed the oatmeal pan. Then she looked at me.

"Holly?" she said. "We'll help, of course. But if you and Annie and Xavier want to plan the party, go for it."

Chapter 4

It was such a crazy morning, I never even got any oatmeal. So Mom and William gave me money to go to Whole Lotta Shakin' for brunch. I invited Xavier and Annie, too.

"I'm going to ask you to do me a favor," I told them on the phone. But I didn't say what it was. This made them curious, and they both said yes.

The name "Whole Lotta Shakin'" is a joke, what William calls a *double entendre*. That is French for "two meanings." I have noticed that when people want to sound smart, they sometimes use a foreign language.

Anyway, the name is supposed to make you think of earthquakes because they happen a lot here in San Francisco. It's also supposed to make you think of Shakespeare. There are pictures of Shakespeare and posters of his plays all over the café.

At noon I went next door to Xavier's house to pick him up. Jim, his dad, answered the door.

"Got a hot date with my kid, huh?" he asked me. "Don't keep him out late, promise? Oh—and watch the caffeine intake. He gets too much, he's a *bear.*"

Jim writes comedy for TV and clubs.

"I'll be careful," I said.

Xavier appeared at the top of the stairs. "Gimme a sec," he said. His voice was funny.

"What's the matter, son?" Jim asked him.

Xavier disappeared back into his room. Jim looked at me.

"I should go up there, huh? That would be the dad thing to do?"

I nodded. Jim went. I worried that Annie would wonder where we were. I didn't worry long because the doorbell rang, and there she was. Annie wore a pink-and-white striped T-shirt under a pink hoodie, with a pair of pink capris. She had her hair pulled back with a thingamabob that was the exact right shade of pink.

"Why are you standing here?" she asked me.

I explained what happened.

"Let's go up there," she said.

The door to Xavier's room was cracked open. Xavier was sitting on his bed. Jim was speaking softly to him. Annie barged in.

"What happened?" she asked. "Are you okay, Dr. X?"

Dr. X is our nickname for Xavier. It comes from when I used to think he was a mad scientist. Now I know he is just a regular boy genius.

Xavier looked up at us. "It's Copernicus," he said. "He's . . . he's—"

"Passed away," Jim said.

Copernicus is Xavier's goldfish.

Annie said, "Let me see," like she didn't believe it. I wondered if she was planning to check the fish's pulse. She looked into the fishbowl. "Oh yeah," she said. "That's dead, all right. But you can get a new one. They have tons at the pet store, you know."

Xavier looked up. "A new one wouldn't be Copernicus," he said.

For a fish, Copernicus was okay. He was shiny and orange. He was a fast swimmer. One time, when George Cat tried to catch him with his paw, he acted pretty brave by not instantly dying of a heart attack.

"Holly?" said Annie. "Maybe you and I should go to Whole Lotta Shakin'. Maybe Dr. X needs time alone? Or time with, uh . . . the corpse of his fish?"

"No, that's okay," Xavier said. "Staying here won't bring Copernicus back."

Chapter 5

Whole Lotta Shakin' is two blocks from my house. Soon we were looking at menus. The barristo guy there, Fred, is my friend. He has a tattoo of a dragonfly on his cheek and a pierced eyebrow. He has a black Mohawk. He dances while he makes espresso. He tells terrible jokes.

"Are you going to get a new goldfish?" Annie asked Xavier.

"I don't want to talk about it," Xavier said.

"Do you want to talk about lunch?" Annie asked.

"I'm going to have a tuna melt," I said.

When I said *tuna*, Xavier's eyes filled with tears.

"I didn't mean that!" I said. "Would you rather I had something else? I like shrimp tempura. Oh shoot."

"A shrimp is not much like a goldfish, Dr. X," Annie said. "It is more like a hermit crab."

Fred came over to take our order. He saw Xavier's sad face and said, "You really need a joke, young man. Do you know this one? A duck walks into a bar and says, 'You got any eggs?'"

"I know it," Xavier said.

"How about this one: Why did the elephant paint its toenails?"

"I know that one, too," Xavier said.

Fred looked at Annie and asked in a loud whisper, "What happened to him?"

"His goldfish died," Annie whispered back.

"No, *really*," Fred said.

"His name was Copernicus," I said.

"Wait right here," Fred said. Then he did a dance step across the floor and into the kitchen. A minute later he came back. He was carrying a shoe box. First I thought it was meant to be a goldfish coffin. Then I realized it had something inside already. Something alive.

"I found him in the alley when I got to work,"

Fred said. "I was going to keep him, but I think you need him more."

I was afraid to look in the box. What lives in an alley anyway? Rats? Mice? Spiders?

Xavier took the box, peeked under the lid, and smiled. "Want to see?" He held out the box to Annie.

She shook her head. "That's okay," she said. "You can just tell me about it, you know?"

"Holly?" he said.

"All right," I said. But I wasn't so sure about this.

"Don't let him out," Fred said. "He's fast."

Carefully I took the box and peeked.

It was a cockroach!

"Ick!" I said. I bobbled the box. It hit the floor. The lid popped off. I thought we were going to spend the next hour jumping on chairs and tables to escape from the runaway cockroach. I thought all the other customers would run outside screaming. I thought Fred would lose his job.

But that isn't what happened.

What happened was the bug stayed in the box. I guess it was in shock. Then Annie saw it, and she cooed, "Oh, a *cricket*!"

And I said, "I knew that."

Xavier thanked Fred. Fred poked some holes in the lid with a chopstick. Then he took our orders. Xavier put the box on the chair next to him.

"Do you really like it?" I asked when Fred was gone.

Xavier shrugged. Annie said, "They're good luck. In China they keep them as pets."

Our food came. I had a sandwich with tofu salad. I don't like tofu so much, but I was afraid anything else would remind Xavier of death. Annie had a raspberry smoothie and a raspberry scone because they matched her outfit. Xavier had chips and guacamole. When the guacamole came it made me think of scum on the inside of a fishbowl. I hoped Xavier didn't think of that, too.

"So what's the favor?" Annie asked.

I explained about the twins' birthday. Xavier and Annie both said they'd like to help. First we needed a theme.

"What's the best birthday party you ever had?" I asked.

"The one where I poked CeCe Mott's tush with a dart," Annie said. "I had a blindfold on. We were playing Pin the Tail on the Donkey. You should've heard CeCe scream. But there wasn't any blood."

"I don't think that will work as a theme," I said. "What about you, Xavier?"

"The Exploratorium," he said.

The Exploratorium is a really great science museum here in San Francisco.

"They're too young for that," I said.

"What do they like?" Xavier asked. "What's their favorite video, Holly?"

"Once Upon a Potty."

Xavier laughed. "Great!" he said. "We can have a potty-themed party! We can have potty games and a potty cake."

Annie scowled.

I wanted to laugh, but I didn't want to annoy Annie. This is the trouble with having friends. Sometimes it's hard keeping them all happy.

I said, "They also like Bill Nye, the Science Guy. They don't understand him, but they like him."

"What if we did something with that?" Xavier asked.

"Dr. X could be Bill Nye!" Annie said. "He could amaze them with science!"

"Guys?" I interrupted.

Xavier was getting excited. "And I could build a sensory-deprivation tube! Like the Exploratorium used to have."

"A what?" Annie said.

"You went in it, and you couldn't see anything or hear anything. It was *so great!*"

"Guys!" I said. "They are only two. Everything amazes them. And sensory deprivation is scary."

Xavier nodded. "That's an even better idea! A *haunted* sensory deprivation tube!"

I tried to argue. But Xavier and Annie had it all figured out. Finally I decided science would be okay. It was for sure better than a potty party.

"What kind of cake is their favorite?" Annie asked.

"They like every kind," I said, "as long as they can spread frosting in their hair. What does Laura like?" Laura is Annie's three-year-old sister.

"White genoise with raspberry ganache and hazelnut buttercream," Annie answered. "You can get it at FrouFrou Bakery."

"My favorite is the kind in the white box next to the donuts," Xavier said.

I told them I wanted to make the cake myself. But I couldn't make genoise. I couldn't even say it. "Is chocolate okay?" I asked.

Annie didn't look sure. But Xavier said, "Sure! With sprinkles!"

We talked about what time the party should be. Mom and William had said it should be after lunch and before dinner. That way we didn't have to serve a whole meal.

"If we have it at one, it's naptime," Annie said.

"That's good," I said. "Fewer people will come."

"Don't we want lots of people?" Xavier asked.

"It will be too crazy," I said.

"So let's invite fewer kids," Xavier said.

"You are clueless," Annie said. "If we invite one preschool friend, we have to invite them all."

"If we don't, a kid might feel bad," I explained.

"They're only two years old!" Xavier said. "They don't know enough to feel bad!"

Walking home, we finished making plans. Xavier was going to come up with amazing science and make the sensory deprivation tube. Annie and I would do decorations. Mom and William had said they would call the parents and make treat bags. We were inviting the twins' preschool class, plus Annie's sister Laura—about fourteen guests plus the twins.

"What if they all say yes?" Annie asked.

"No way," I said. "One o'clock is naptime!"

Chapter 6

I turned out to be wrong.

By Wednesday, all the guests had RSVP'd.

And they were all coming!

We needed reinforcements. That means we needed help. So on Wednesday afternoon I called my friends Sylvie and Kimmi.

Kimmi said no problem, she would be there.

Sylvie asked, "Why does Dr. X get to do all the science? Girls can do science."

I said, "Obviously girls can do science. But Xavier volunteered."

Sylvie said, "I'll help if I get to do science."

I said, "Great," but I was kind of lying. I was

afraid Xavier wouldn't like sharing his show with Sylvie. I went over to his house to explain.

At most of my friends' houses, you don't ring the doorbell between five and seven o'clock. Some of them would be having a family dinner together. The rest would be at soccer or piano or ballet.

But Xavier is a boy genius. Boy geniuses don't have time for regular-kid activities. And his family's idea of dinner together is sharing a bag of garlic-and-onion chips.

Jim answered the door. He was wearing a headset. He looked part spaceman and part ESPN. He mouthed, "Hi, Holly. Sorry. Phone." Then he waved me up the stairs. Xavier was sitting on the floor in his room. He was eating a tub of rice pudding.

"Qu-Ming likes it," he said.

"Chew-Ming?" I repeated.

"Q-u-M-i-n-g." Xavier spelled it, then nodded at a cage on the table next to him. "He has real potential. Good teeth."

What was Xavier talking about?

I knelt so I could look into the cage. "Oh, the cricket! What do you mean he has potential? Oh *gross*! You're sharing pudding with a *bug*!"

With his finger, Xavier put a grain of rice on a blade of grass. Then he poked it into the cage. The cricket clenched it between his jaws. *Yuck.*

"Don't call him a *bug*," Xavier said. "He's a fighting cricket. A future champion. He has to be on a very strict diet. Rice and dead flies."

"Do you share dead flies with him, too?"

Xavier spooned pudding into his own mouth. "That would be gross," he said. Then he held the tub out to me. "Want some?"

"*No!*"

"You don't have to be rude." Xavier gave the cricket another grain.

"What was that you said about him? How he could be a champion?"

Xavier nodded. "People all over the world stage cricket fights. If I can get Qu-Ming bulked up on pudding, he could be worth a lot of money."

"How do you know he wants to fight?" I asked.

Xavier studied the cricket. "He does have kind of a gentle face. Maybe he could be a singing cricket. They're worth money, too. Only he hasn't sung a single note so far. And I don't have much time to train him. They only live three months."

"Maybe he'll be like Copernicus and live a long time," I said.

Xavier replaced the lid on the rice pudding tub. "We had Copernicus's funeral yesterday."

"I would have come if you'd told me," I said.

Xavier said there was only enough room for immediate family.

That sounded weird. "Why?" I asked.

"Our bathroom's not that big," he said.

It took me a second to figure out why you would have a funeral in the bathroom. "You mean you flushed—?"

Xavier nodded. "Each of us said something nice about him. I said he wasn't a bit yucky. Jim said he was easily worth twice as much as we paid for him."

"How much did you pay for him?" I asked.

"A quarter," Xavier said. "Then we threw flower petals in, and away he went."

I guess a bathroom funeral is better than no funeral. Xavier seemed to be feeling better.

I realized it was getting late, and I had better tell him the real reason I came over. "What would you think if Sylvie did science at the party, too?" I asked.

Xavier said, "That would be good. I could use a lovely assistant."

"Uh . . . that isn't what I meant," I said. "Sylvie wants to do her *own* amazing science."

Xavier frowned. "Do I still get top billing?"

"What do you mean?" I asked.

"Like on TV. The biggest star gets top billing."

Sometimes I think Xavier is crazy. "This isn't TV. It's a birthday party for two-year-olds."

"Every show biz career starts somewhere," Xavier said.

"How about if Sylvie is special guest star?" I asked.

"It's a deal," Xavier agreed.

I walked home. I was thinking friends are almost as much trouble as twins.

Chapter 7

Thursday night I couldn't sleep. It was two days till the twins' birthday. I was all stressed out.

Marcy, my stepmother, makes a list when she can't sleep. So I bumped the cats onto the floor, turned on my light, and this is what I wrote:

1) shop for cake ingredients
2) make cake
3) frost cake
4) bug Xavier about sensory deprivation tube
5) help Annie decorate
6) *do not* lose party guests

I turned the light off. The cats jumped back up on the bed and settled in. Soon they were purring.

All except for George. He was snoring. I still did not fall asleep. I started thinking. Before the twins, Mom and William and I did fun things. We played at the beach. We ate dim sum in Chinatown. We went to the teahouse in Golden Gate Park. We bought gelato in Little Italy.

But now when I want to do something, Mom and William say, "Oh honey, we're too tired."

There is something else about twins. Everybody thinks they are so great for no reason except there's two of them. Like sometimes if I'm out with them, strangers say, *"Awwww, aren't they precious?"* And I think, What am I? The amazing, invisible big sister?

When I woke up, I was cranky. But then the twins turned out to be funny and good at breakfast. Jeremy took his pink medicine, no problem. Dylan tried to feed me his applesauce. The trouble with twins is just when you're mad at them, they turn all cute on you.

After school we were going to the grocery store.

First we had to wrestle the boys into their car seats. This is hard because the boys are squirmy. Also because our garage is small. You can't even open the car doors all the way.

Mom finally buckled Jeremy in. I was buckling Dylan. Mom said, *"Ouch! Darn that thing!"*

"What happened?" I asked.

Mom pointed to the padlock on one of the garage cupboards. "I bumped it and bruised my bottom," she said.

The boys thought this was a laugh riot. "Mommy got a bottom!" Jeremy shouted, and soon Dylan joined him: "Mommy bottom!"

In the car I said, "What does William keep locked in that cupboard anyway?"

Mom shrugged. "I don't know. But he says it isn't dangerous."

At the store, Mom got a cart and I got a cart. Then Mom got a boy and I got a boy. Mine was Jeremy.

Mom and Dylan were getting punch and little toys for treat bags. Jeremy and I were getting cake ingredients. But on the way we had to stop at the live lobster tank. Jeremy likes to watch them climb over each other. He thinks they are pets. I don't tell him the awful truth.

In the baking aisle, we found the flour, sugar, oil, and birthday candles.

"Two candles for Jeremy," I said. "Two candles for Dylan."

Jeremy grinned. "I be two yea's o'd!" Then he said, "Get down now, Hah-wee?"

Sometimes I can read Jeremy's mind. What was in it right then was gummy worms. The store keeps them in a bin at two-year-old level.

I made faces to distract him. Then we played Freeway. That's where you run with the cart and make honking and siren noises. I was tired out when we spotted Mom and Dylan by the toilet paper. Jeremy got all excited. He remembered the great TP confetti war.

"Want dat!" He pointed at a jumbo-size package.

"So you can make a jumbo-size mess," I said.

"*Yeah!*" Jeremy said.

Mom grabbed the package. "We need some anyway," she said. "We seem to be using a lot lately."

We went to checkout. I put my groceries in Mom's cart and let Dylan and Jeremy get down. They looked at the magazines.

"What dis?" Dylan pointed to a movie star's low-cut dress.

"It's skin," I said. "Everybody has skin. See?" I pulled up his shirt and tickled him. Meanwhile Jeremy looked at a cooking magazine.

"Cake!" he said. "Butday cake?"

Mom was in the self-service line. The machine refused to scan the espresso she wanted for William. A red light was flashing. We were stuck.

"Weed sto-wy, Hah-wee." Jeremy handed me the cooking magazine.

"Butday sto-wy," Dylan said.

"It's not time for a story," I said. "There are people behind us in line."

"Dey wait," Jeremy said.

The red light kept flashing. "Once upon a time," I began, "there were two charming boys named Dylan and Jeremy."

Dylan looked at Jeremy. "Dy-wun is *my* name!" he said.

Jeremy pointed at himself. "Germy!" he said.

"What a coincidence!" I said. "Also Dylan and Jeremy had a sister named Holly. She was kind and smart and beautiful. She made Dylan and Jeremy the best birthday cake yet. They said thank you a million times. And they were good forever. The end!"

"Good sto-wy!" Dylan said.

"Good story," said the man behind us in line. "You wouldn't by chance be Holly?"

I turned jelly red. I didn't know anybody else was listening. I wanted to tell him I know better stories, but it was time to go.

"Come on." Mom headed for the exit. I tagged along, a twin holding each hand. When Mom hit the parking lot, she raised her hands over her head and cheered: *"Woo-hoo! We survived another trip to the grocery store!"*

"Woo-hoo!" The boys copied her—and we all high-fived.

Chapter 8

After dinner came the following disaster:

The boys wanted to help make the cake.

"They'll lose interest fast," Mom said. "Don't worry."

I worried.

Three cats were in the kitchen. Boo was asleep by the refrigerator. George was curled up in William's chair. Max was in the doorway. Max likes doorways in case he needs to escape.

The boys climbed up on step stools. I gave them each a plastic bowl, a wooden spoon, and some water to pour back and forth. They did this for thirty seconds. Then they figured out they were not making the cake.

This is another trouble with the twins. They are smart when they want to be.

"Gimme dat?" Jeremy asked. "Peez, Hah-wee." He wanted the flour.

"Yummy!" Dylan said. "Tokit!" He could smell the cocoa. "Gimme? Peez?"

"Doesn't taste good," I said.

Dylan and Jeremy looked at each other. Was I lying, or was I stupid? It was *tokit*! Of *course* it tasted good! *"Peez!?"* they said together.

I shrugged and gave them each a tiny spoonful. They grinned till the taste hit their tongues. Then they frowned and tried to spit. I wiped their faces and tongues with paper towels.

"Didn't I tell you it was bitter?" I said. "But now we add sugar."

Jeremy said, *"Sugar! Yummy!"* And he opened his mouth for me to pour it down his throat.

"We don't eat plain sugar," I said.

"Why, Hah-wee?" Dylan asked. "Yike sugar."

I told them plain sugar is bad for you. Saying it, I thought how this cake-baking deal is strange. First you put in horrible bitter stuff. Then you put in stuff that's bad for you.

"I promise it will be good when it's done," I told them. I cracked an egg.

"Me do!" Jeremy said. Breaking something is his kind of fun.

"Isn't it time for you to lose interest?" I said.

They shook their heads no. So I recited:

Humpty Dumpty sat on a wall.
Humpty Dumpty had a great fall.
All the king's horses and all the king's men
Couldn't put Humpty together again.

"Say 'gain, Hah-wee?" Jeremy begged.

So I repeated it. And repeated it. And then all the eggs were cracked.

"Enough with the Humpty," I said. "Do you want to stir? After that, we combine ingredients."

I should have been better prepared. I should have held onto the bowls. But making the cake was taking forever. I wanted to get it done.

I handed each boy a bowl and turned away. All I wanted was the rubber scraper from the drawer. It took two seconds to get it.

Two seconds too long.

Clatter. "Uh-oh," said Jeremy.

Clatter. "Uh-oh," said Dylan.

I turned around. The cake ingredients were now combining on the floor. The cats figure any-

thing on the floor belongs to them. Tails swishing, Boo, George, and Max tiptoed toward the sticky sugar-flour mess. Wilbur's sense of smell brought him into the kitchen, too. This time he didn't have toilet paper in his mouth. He had Patrick Opossum's tail. The rest of Patrick Opossum followed along behind.

Max meowed at the cake ingredients but kept his distance.

Boo thought an egg yolk was a mouse. He batted it, and it slid away. He wiggled his rear end and pounced.

George decided if Boo wanted it, the egg yolk must be good. So he jumped on Boo. Boo twisted onto his back to fight George off. They both forgot the egg yolk. They were too busy rolling in unmixed cake batter.

The twins laughed and pointed. But then Wilbur dragged Patrick Opossum into the middle of it all. Now we had chocolate-covered opossum—and chocolate-covered cats.

Jeremy shook his head. "Ki'ies aw di'ty!"

Dylan made a face. "Patwick aw di'ty, too!"

I stomped my foot and shouted, *"Scat!"*

But what a mistake! Wilbur dropped Patrick Opossum and ran. The other cats ran in every direction—spreading the mess in every direction, too.

The twins started laughing again. Making the cake had turned out to be even more fun than they expected! I was not laughing. I was trying to remember why I ever volunteered to do this anyway.

Chapter 9

Mom and I cleaned up. Then she got the twins ready for bed. William went to 7-Eleven to buy more cocoa. I started another cake. It was way past bedtime when it came out of the oven.

The next day was Saturday, party day!

In the morning I frosted the cake and made punch. Mom and William stuffed treat bags and put food out for parents. The parents were supposed to be in the kitchen or on the back deck. The party was in the backyard.

At noon Xavier and Jim brought over the sensory-deprivation tube. It was silver and about four feet wide. It looked sturdy. It had a wooden door attached with a hinge. Inside there was soft, green, foamy stuff.

"That's what makes it feel like you're floating," Xavier explained. "Also it helps with soundproofing."

When Sylvie, Kimmi, and Annie arrived, we crawled in to try it out. Boo came, too. We were squished.

"It doesn't work," Sylvie said. "I can still feel my bottom against the cold ground."

"I can feel Boo's claws kneading my tummy," I said.

"I can hear you talking," Kimmi said.

"I think we're not supposed to talk," I said.

"Tell Boo to stop purring," Sylvie said.

Boo kept purring, but nobody talked. It was true. I couldn't hear anything from outside. And it was so dark I couldn't see my hand in front of my face.

"I can still smell," Kimmi said. "I smell frosting."

"The frosting is me," I told her. "I licked the beaters this morning."

"I'm hot," Annie said. "Plus we have to finish the balloons."

"Let's get him to let us out of here then," I said. "*Xavier?*"

Nothing happened.

I knocked on the inside of the door. *"Xavier! Let us out!"* Nothing happened again.

We looked at each other. I mean, it was too dark for us to *see* each other, but we looked where we thought we were. "Let's all scream at the same time," I said.

"What should we scream?" Annie asked.

"What if we all scream 'help'?" I said.

"I don't think it's that bad yet," Annie said.

"Annie is right," Kimmi said.

"Okay." I was exasperated. "Let's scream: 'Let us out!'"

"Okay," Annie and Kimmi agreed.

"One-two-three," I said.

"Let us out!" we all screamed.

The door popped open. "You don't have to scream," Xavier said. "It's not soundproof from the outside. I didn't have that much acoustic buffering. But still, it's pretty cool, isn't it?"

We crawled out. I raised my hand to high-five Xavier. He didn't high-five back. "What's the matter?" I asked. "Are you sad because it isn't totally soundproof?"

"Or smell-proof?" Annie said. "We could smell Holly, you know."

"That's not it," Xavier said. "I'm sad about Qu-Ming."

"Uh-oh," I said. "Is he dead, too?"

Xavier shook his head. "He's gone."

"That's better than dead," Sylvie said.

"Yesterday I got a special cage for him in Chinatown," Xavier explained. "The holes must have been too big. Now every time I take a step I'm afraid I'll squash him."

"Maybe Wilbur could find him," I said. "He's good at catching bugs."

"What does Wilbur do when he gets one?" Xavier asked.

"He . . ." I started to say. "He eats them. Never mind."

Mom came down the steps into the backyard.

"I finally got the twins down for their nap," she said. "Unfortunately it took longer than I thought. They're sound asleep, and the party starts in twenty minutes."

I had worried it might rain. I had worried I might burn the cake. But I never worried the twins would sleep through their own birthday party!

I sighed. "Another disaster."

Chapter 10

Mom thought I was being too dramatic.

"They can sleep a few minutes," Mom said. "Then we'll wake them."

We still had three balloons to blow up when guests started to arrive. Soon little kids were swarming around like ants.

"The first thing we do is count them," Annie said. "That way at the end we'll know how many are missing."

"None will be missing!" I said. "We have name tags to keep them straight. We just need to round them up and tag them."

"Oh, that's easy," Sylvie said. Then she

whooped, "Yippee-yi-ti-yay!" and started galloping around slapping name tags on kids. The kids ran and whooped, too.

"How does she know she's getting the right tag on the right kid?" Kimmi asked.

"She doesn't," Annie said. "My sister Laura is now called 'Kelton.' "

Laura, aka Kelton, was tugging at my T-shirt. "Where are Dy'wun and Germy?" she asked.

"S'eeping," I said. "I mean *sleeping*."

"I wake dem up," Laura said.

"I wake dem up, too," a black-haired boy said. According to the tag, his name was Jessica.

"Mom thinks it's better if they sleep a little longer," I told them.

A little girl who was not Laura, but who had Laura's name tag, said, "Me come, too."

She and the boy started for the house. Meanwhile Xavier and Sylvie were announcing amazing science. Kimmi was taping balloons to the fence. Annie was trying to find the mom of a crying boy. Out of the corner of my eye, I saw a girl heading out of the yard. I caught up with her. "Hi," I said. "Where are you going?"

"Home," she answered.

I tried to reason with her. There would be

cake. There would be games. This was going to be some *fun* party!

She kept walking. I looked up on the deck where the parents were. Mom was talking to another mom. She looked down at me and smiled. I didn't want to ask for help. It was supposed to be *my* party for the twins.

Xavier yelled, *"Holly! Can you come here, please?"*

I didn't know what else to do, so I scooped the little girl up. That's what I do with Dylan and Jeremy. She screamed and wiggled. She was heavy. It was only very good luck that I didn't drop her on her head. I brought her over to the card table where Sylvie was doing science.

Sylvie lifted a chain of paper clips out of a top hat using a magnet. Then she looked up, smiled a big smile, and said: *"Amazing!"*

But her audience was gone.

"Where did they go?" she asked me.

"Help!" Xavier called again.

"Keep an eye on this one." I put the wiggling girl down by Sylvie. "She tends to escape."

I ran over to Xavier. He had been doing amazing soap bubbles. But he had lost his audience, too. They were much more interested in Lev, probably not his real name, who had brought a loaded squirt gun to the party.

What kind of parents would let a kid do that?

Lev had very good aim. He had already shot Xavier. This caused Xavier to spill his tub of soap, which created a very slippery mud puddle. Several kids had grabbed plastic spoons and forks so they could dig in the mud.

The mess was unbelievable. On the other hand, the kids were having an excellent time.

Sylvie and Xavier gave up on science and helped me herd kids. Every once in a while, a parent would come down from the deck and tell us what a great job we were doing. These parents must be blind, I thought. But I didn't argue.

Laura came up to me. "Where da c'own, Hahwee?" she asked.

"We don't have a clown. We have science," I said.

Laura shook her head. "Dis is a *bad* butday party," she said.

I kind of agreed. But what could we do to make it better?

"The sensory-deprivation tube!" Kimmi said.

"Good idea," I said. "They'll be safe in there." I told the kids to line up, and they did. Lining up was something they were good at.

"We should do a kid count," Annie said. "While we can see them all."

"She's right," Kimmi said.

We counted. There used to be fourteen. Now there were twelve.

"That's not bad," Xavier said. "We've still got more than seventy-five percent."

"Didn't two kids go to wake up Dylan and Jeremy?" Sylvie asked.

Oh my gosh! I totally forgot Dylan and Jeremy! I sprinted up the stairs and into the house. In the kitchen Mom asked if everything was okay. She had to talk loud because the espresso pot was gurgling.

I didn't want Mom to worry. "Everything's fine," I said. "Uh . . . you didn't see a couple of kids run by here, did you?"

"You mean you can't find them?" Mom said.

I didn't answer directly. "There are five responsible big kids out there, Mom. Not to mention most of the parents are still here."

"That's what I—" Mom started to say, but she

was interrupted by an explosion. It came from the stove. It was the espresso pot. A brown fountain of boiling espresso spray shot everywhere.

Everybody in the kitchen ducked for cover. But then they realized they were okay, and they started to laugh.

I still had to find the kids. I ran up the stairs. I burst into the twins' room.

Here is the good news: All four kids were there, and none of them were crying.

Here is the bad news: The room was a spider-web of toilet paper. It was wrapped around the bedposts, hanging from the lamps and picture frames, covering all the toys.

The kids were sitting on the floor. They were having a great time. They were wrapping Boo Cat in toilet paper. He looked like a cat mummy. An unhappy cat mummy.

"Yook, Hah-wee, aw piddy!" Jeremy waved his hands to show their newly decorated room.

"Beautiful," I said. "Why don't you let Boo go now and come to the party?"

"No!" Dylan shook his head.

"We hate da potty," Jeremy said.

"*Not* potty! Party!" I said. "Your birthday

party, remember? It's going on without you in the backyard. Everybody's having a *great* time," I added.

Still covered in white, Boo sprinted away. The kids and I trooped down the stairs and through the kitchen. Mom was on the floor wiping up espresso puddles. William was on the phone.

"Do you do deliveries?" he asked. "It's an emergency."

Outside, the line for the tube was gone. A couple of kids were playing in the mud. Annie, Sylvie, Kimmi, and Xavier were cleaning up the science.

"Where did the rest of the kids go?" I asked.

Sylvie nodded. "In the tube."

"All of them?"

"It was the safest place," she said. "They can't escape, and we can get this stuff cleaned up."

"How long have they been in there?" I asked. "What if they suffocate?"

Xavier looked at his watch. "With current atmospheric pressure, there should be enough oxygen for three more minutes. Give or take."

I ran over to the tube and opened it. Uh-oh. It was *very* quiet inside.

Then—*what a relief*—I heard giggles and whispers.

"Shhh!" a little kid said. "S'eeping."

Sure enough, two of the kids were curled up like cats.

Of course now Dylan and Jeremy wanted their turn in the tube. And we had to wake up the nappers. They were pretty cranky. I expected another disaster.

But rescue was on the way.

"C'own's coming!" Laura called out.

"But there isn't any—*oh*." I said.

Chapter 11

"Never fear! Espresso's here!" Dancing his way into the backyard was Fred. He carried a tray loaded with cardboard cups from Whole Lotta Shakin'. Fred is a colorful dresser. Today he wore orange boots, green jeans, a Hawaiian shirt, and a yellow tie.

I could see how Laura might think he was a clown.

"I was on my way home anyway," Fred told me. "So I told William I'd drop these off." But before he could do that, a bunch of knee-high party guests rushed him. Amazingly Fred didn't spill a drop. "Greetings, babies!" he said. "Would you like to hear a joke?"

The little kids fell to the grass in a neat semi-circle. They didn't know about science. But they knew about storytime.

"Just one joke," Fred said. "I have a very important delivery to make."

"I'll take the coffee," I said. "You tell the joke."

"Why wouldn't the skeleton go to the movies?" I heard Fred ask as I climbed the steps. The kids squealed with laughter.

"That wasn't the joke," Fred explained. "That was the *setup*. See, babies, a riddle comes in two parts: setup and punch line. Shall we try it again?"

William's eyes lit up when I walked into the kitchen. It took a minute for us to sort out the orders. When that was done, Mom asked, "What happened to Fred?"

"Kidnapped," I said. "Take a look."

Mom and William joined the other parents on the deck. From there they could see Fred telling stories to their delighted kids. Several kids were sucking their thumbs. One had a finger up his nose.

". . . so the wolf said to Red Riding Hood, 'I'll huff and I'll puff and I'll blow your house into the bay!'" Fred was saying. Then he turned to Xavier. "Is that how it goes?"

Xavier nodded. "Close enough."

"But right then," Fred went on, "who should walk in the door but Glinda, Good Witch of the North! Needless to say, the wolf was *flummoxed*!"

Fred's story continued—and now the parents were listening, too. In the end, the dish ran away with the spoon, and everyone else lived happily ever after in Honolulu.

"And what do you think the moral is?" Fred asked.

"Wolves are people, too?" Kimmi tried.

"Well, *that*," Fred said. "But in addition: Black-and-white is always more flattering than color. Now who's for cake?"

"Coming right up!" I said.

"I'll help," Mom said.

Kimmi, Annie, Xavier, and Sylvie followed us into the kitchen. I ordered them around. "Cups! Napkins! Punch! Ice cream!"

The cake was in the dining room. As Mom and I went in, Wilbur Cat came out. He had frosting on his whiskers.

"Oh no," I moaned.

But actually: Oh yes. He hadn't eaten the whole cake. He had only licked off the frosting and taken bites around the edges.

"Maybe I could cover the bite marks with frosting?" I said to Mom.

"Holly!" Mom said.

"Okay. Bad idea," I said. But I didn't have another idea. There were sixteen kids waiting for birthday cake. Now we didn't have birthday cake.

Luckily William had drunk his espresso. He felt like a superhero. He saw the cake and said, "I have just the thing."

Chapter 12

Mom didn't think the locked cupboard in the garage held anything dangerous. But she was wrong. It *was* dangerous. Dangerous to William's tummy.

All along William had kept a stash of his favorite food in that cupboard. It was supposed to be in case of earthquake or other emergency.

William's favorite food is Twinkies. This was an emergency.

We worked very fast. I washed the cake plate. William lined up Twinkies to form a rectangle. Mom squirted whipped cream on the Twinkies. Then she spread it with a knife.

The result looked like a plain white frosted cake.

"Needs something," William said. "Do we have sprinkles?"

Mom found some. "They're pretty old," she said.

"No one ever died from an old sprinkle," William said.

William sprinkled the cake. Mom put two candles on one end for Jeremy and two on the other end for Dylan. William lit them. "Ready?" he asked. We brought the cake outside. Everybody sang "Happy Birthday." Dylan and Jeremy sang, too. They had big silly grins on their faces.

After the song it got quiet. In the quiet I heard something: *Chirp-chirp*. The sound was familiar. But what was it?

Xavier knew. "Qu-Ming!" He dropped to his knees and started looking everywhere in the grass.

"Qu-Ming was singing 'Happy Birthday!'" I said.

"How do you know it was 'Happy Birthday'?" Annie asked.

"He'll get squashed for sure," Xavier said, "Everybody sit still! Sing another chorus or something."

Out of the corner of my eye, I saw Wilbur Cat. He was under a picnic bench, wiggling his rump, getting ready to attack. But attack what? Oh no! Had he spotted Qu-Ming? Where *was* Qu-Ming?

"B'ow canduhs?" Dylan asked.

"Yes, honey, go ahead and blow out the candles!" Mom said. Then she nodded at Xavier on the ground. "What's with him?" she asked me.

"He's looking for his pet cricket," I whispered. I was still watching Wilbur. Wilbur's tail was swishing.

Mom cut the cake. "Pet cricket?" she said. Then she handed a boy a plate with cake on it. Reading his name tag, she said, "Here you go . . . Jessica?"

The boy took the plate. It tilted. The cake fell. Wilbur chose the same moment to spring. The cake landed on Wilbur, who yowled and dashed away. He had a big glob of whipped cream on his ear.

Chirp-chirp-chirp-chirp.

"Qu-Ming?" Xavier picked up the boy's cake.

"Mine!" The boy grabbed for it.

"You can have a new piece," I told him. "You don't want that one. It's all covered with . . ." I was going to say grass, but then I saw something.

Was it my imagination? Or did the whipped cream *move*?

With his fingers, Xavier dissected the cake. Then from out of the frosting, crawled a little brown-winged body.

"Qu-Ming!" Xavier said.

"How do you know?" Annie said. "He's so covered in whipped cream he could be anybody."

Fred peered at the bug. "That's him," he said. "See? He recognizes me. I've always had good rapport with bugs."

"And he's learned to sing!" said Xavier. "What a smart bug you are! Now I can turn you into a champion for sure!"

"He needs a bath," Annie said.

"How do you give a cricket a bath?" Kimmi asked.

"Google it," Sylvie said.

"I have a better idea," said Annie. "Where's the kid with the squirt gun?"

Dr. X covered Qu-Ming with his hands. "No way!"

After cake came presents. Dylan's and Jeremy's eyes got huge when they saw so many. They ripped wrapping paper, tore boxes, put ribbon on their heads. They didn't care what was in the boxes. The outsides were fun enough.

The cats agreed. Wilbur tried to eat a stick-on bow, which stuck on to his head. Max stalked a wad of tissue paper, but Boo pounced on it first. Max tried to steal it back from Boo. But Lev—the kid with the squirt gun—shot it out of the way. Boo chased it and got squirted. He had to give himself an emergency bath. Meanwhile George got the wad of paper and took a big bite. Then he let go and looked up at me. He was disappointed it didn't taste like a kitty treat.

The cats and the boys thought the presents were fun. The party guests didn't. Some cried because the presents weren't for them. Some tried to swipe presents. Then the twins cried.

It was Fred who stepped in and said, "Presents are all done!"

Annie and I and Sylvie whisked everything out of the way. Fred distracted the kids. "I can make a handkerchief disappear!" He pulled a napkin out of his pocket, waved it in the air, and stuffed it up his sleeve. "Voilà!" he said.

The kids oohed and aahed—except for Laura. She pointed to his arm. "In dere," she said.

Fred nodded and smiled. *"Is right!"* he cried.

Then he pulled the napkin out and waved it some more. The little kids oohed and aahed and clapped.

Finally it was time for the guests to leave.

"Great party, kids," a mom said to me as she and her son left. "He had a *wonderful* time!" The boy, whose name tag said 'Max,' was covered with mud and whipped cream, plus he was whimpering. But I didn't want to argue.

When I thought all the kids and parents had left, Mom came up to me. "We seem to be missing one," she said. I saw that a dad was standing behind her.

"About yay big?" He held his hand at thigh height. "With freckles."

I turned around and scanned the backyard.

"Can you be a bit more specific, sir?" Xavier asked. "A lot of kids have freckles."

"Dr. X?" Annie said. "I think if we find any stray kid with freckles, it's a good bet it's the right one."

We were getting ready to look when I thought of something. Our backyard is not that big. There are no mine shafts or hollow tree trunks. There was really only one place a kid could disappear into.

I opened the sensory-deprivation tube. Out walked George. "Hello-o-o-o?" I called inside.

"Peekaboo," a small voice answered. "I see you!"

"Got him!" I called.

The dad jogged over. "Does he have freckles?"

"Freckles," I said. "Check."

The little boy held up his arms to be carried. "Cake?" he asked.

"I'll get you a takeout order." A minute later, I handed it to them along with his treat bag. "I hope he had a good time," I said.

"I think he had a good nap," the dad said. "See you next year!"

Uh-oh, I thought. We don't really have to do this again, do we?

Chapter 13

Finally everybody went home.

I collapsed on the sofa.

"Those were the longest two hours of my life," I told Mom and William.

"We'll clean up," Mom said. "You relax."

Unfortunately the boys came in to help me relax. After them came the cats. They all piled on top of me.

"What do you say we take a nap together?" I asked.

"Not s'eepy," Dylan said. Then he yawned, and Jeremy stuck his thumb in his mouth.

We were falling off to sleep—cats, twins, and me—when the phone rang. We jumped, then settled back. Mom came in a minute later. When she saw my eyes were open, she held out the phone.

"Your father," she mouthed.

I took the phone carefully, trying not to make earthquakes for twins or cats.

"Hi Dad," I whispered.

"What's the matter?" he asked.

I explained why I was whispering. Dad laughed. "I'm glad you're such a good big sister, Holly, because . . . well, guess what? I have some news. That is, Marcy and I have some news."

Sometimes I am as dim as a bulb can get and still stay lit. I should have known what was coming, but I was too tired to think. "What?" I asked.

"We're going to have a baby!" he said.

"Oh Dad," I said without thinking, "I hope it's not twins."

Dad laughed. We talked a little more. After we hung up, I closed my eyes and fell asleep. I dreamed I was tied to a chair with toilet paper. Dylan woke me by pulling my hair. Boo was kneading my belly with his front paws; Wilbur was nibbling my socks.

"Good mo'ning, Hah-wee," Jeremy said.

"Good morning, Jeremy," I said.

Dylan rubbed his eyes and took one last suck on his thumb. "Heh-wo, Hah-wee."

I put one arm around each of them. They were warm and soft. They smelled like cake. They were smiling.

"I love you, you guys. You know that?" I said.

At dinnertime, there were wineglasses on the table.

I held mine up. "What's this for?" I asked.

"We are celebrating!" William said.

I couldn't believe it. Hadn't we had enough birthday?

Mom came up beside William. He put his arm around her. "Tonight," William began, "we celebrate Holly Garland—world's greatest big sister!"

I was totally surprised.

"We're having your favorite dinner," Mom said, "duck with plum sauce. I got it from Szechuan Sushi."

"I *hate* duck," Jeremy said.

"Then you may have rice," Mom told him.

She poured wine for herself and William. She poured sparkling grape juice for me. The boys got juice, too. They did not get wineglasses. I guess there are a few good things about being the big kid.

We all sat down. Mom said, "Thank you, Holly. You did a splendid job today. Your little brothers are lucky to have you for a sister."

"And we're lucky to have you for a daughter," William said. "It's been a little wild here lately. . . ."

"And things aren't likely to get easier soon," Mom added.

"But we love each other. That's the main thing." William wiped his eye, and Jeremy said, "Daddy c'ying."

"Way c'ying," Dylan agreed.

"I am not," William said. "A speck of dust is all."

Before bed, I called my dad back. "I shouldn't have said what I said," I told him.

"What was that?" Dad asked.

"How I hope Marcy doesn't have twins?" I said, "Really, Dad, twins are okay. It's only—"

"—only what?" Dad asked.

"Only that till you kind of get used to them, they're a whole lot of trouble."